Living with My Stepfather
Is Like Living with a Moose

Living with
My Stepfather
Is Like Living with a Moose

Lynea Bowdish

PICTURES BY **Blanche Sims**

FARRAR STRAUS GIROUX   NEW YORK

Library of Congress Cataloging-in-Publication Data
Bowdish, Lynea.
Living with my stepfather is like living with a moose / Lynea Bowdish ;
pictures by Blanche Sims. — 1st ed.
p.   cm.
Summary: Athletically talented Matt finds it difficult to accept his new
klutzy stepfather.
ISBN 0-374-34630-5
[1. Stepfathers—Fiction.]   I. Sims, Blanche, ill.   II. Title.
PZ7.B67194Li   1997   [Fic]—dc20   96-21313

For my niece and nephews,
Elise, Craig, and Kyle,
with love

Living with My Stepfather
Is Like Living with a Moose

Chapter One

My stepfather is a klutz. When he and Mom got married two months ago, he dropped the ring. It rolled across the judge's office and probably into the air vent. We all got down on the floor to look for it. It wasn't any use. Mom said she didn't like wearing rings, anyway.

Now that Frank's living with us, we never know what's going to happen. He knocks over milk glasses. He spills sugar. He cuts himself when he tries to help fix dinner.

Frank's a manager in a supermarket. He must break half of what's in the store.

Three times this week, he stepped on Juliet's tail. But beagles are smart. She learned to go behind the couch until he sits down. Then she comes out and jumps into his lap. She lets him scratch her long brown ears. I can't figure out what she sees in him.

I can't figure out what Mom sees in him, either. When he bumps into her or steps on her foot, she just laughs. She laughs a lot lately. I should be glad about that. She didn't laugh much before Frank.

The first time we met, he told me to call him Frank.

"Call me Frank," he said, and stumbled over the little rug in front of the big chair. He didn't seem much taller than I am. The light

4

glistened off his bald head. He looked like Humpty Dumpty.

Mom might have had something to do with my calling him Frank. She knows I wouldn't call anyone Dad.

My father died before I could remember him. But it's not as if he hasn't been around. I go through the pictures a lot. He was tall, like me, with dark hair and brown eyes. And his name was Matthew, like mine. In most of the pictures, he's playing sports.

Mom says I take after him that way, too. I'm on three teams at Dent Elementary School—soccer, basketball, and softball. I'm one of the best players in the fifth grade. Someday I'm going to play professional basketball or baseball. It depends on how tall I get. And if I can live that long with Frank around. Without injuries, I mean.

"You're crazy to complain," my friend Toby said one day after school.

We were going through our matchbook collections. I have 36. Toby has 105. That's because his father travels a lot. We save the covers. The matches go to our mothers to get rid of.

"Half the kids in our class would give any-thing for a stepfather like yours," Toby said. "He's not mean. He doesn't have a bunch of kids. And he leaves you alone."

I grunted. It's easy for Toby to talk. He has a storybook family: a mother, a father, and a little sister.

Toby's only problem is his sister. He says she's almost as tall as he is. She's two. It's not true, of course. Toby's a little self-conscious about his height. He's sort of short.

"Frank's always bumping into things," I said. "It's like living with a moose."

Toby shrugged. "Your mother seems to like him."

"My mother gets weird ideas," I said.

"Now she says Frank and I should be in the father-son softball game at school."

"What's wrong with that?" Toby asked.

I laughed. "Can you imagine Frank playing ball? He can hardly hold his knife and fork without stabbing himself. But I've got a few weeks to get out of it."

"How about trading this Sleepy Inn cover for your China Cookin'?" Toby said.

I ignored him. He's always trying to trade his Sleepy Inns. That's where his father stays.

Toby doesn't understand the way I feel. Neither does Mom. She's forever asking questions.

"How are you and Frank getting along?" she'll ask.

Or, "Why don't you and Frank go for a walk?"

Or, "Why don't you and Frank watch that new show on TV?"

I know what she's trying to do, but I can't

help it. Frank and I have nothing in common.

The following Saturday, Mom did it again. "Why not take Frank bowling today?" she asked.

I love to bowl. But bowling with Frank didn't seem safe. Or smart.

"You mean, where all the kids can see us?" I said.

"He *is* your stepfather," Mom said, her voice getting deep. It does that when she gets mad. "He's nothing to be ashamed of. I think it's a good idea. You and Frank will go bowling this afternoon. Together."

The way she said it, I knew she meant it.

Frank was in the living room, reading one of his bird-watching magazines. Before Frank, I didn't know people really watched birds. I thought it was a joke. Juliet lay stretched across his lap.

"Mom thinks we should go bowling this afternoon," I said.

"That sounds like fun," Frank said.

He put down the magazine and stroked Juliet's ears. She made the little purring noise she makes when she's content. She sounds like a cat.

"I didn't know your mother likes to bowl."

"She doesn't," I said. "She wants the two of us to go."

"Does your mother realize I don't know how to bowl?"

I tried not to sigh with relief. Maybe Toby would want to go to the movies.

"Matt will teach you how," Mom said, coming into the room.

"I'm willing to try it if Matt is," Frank said.

So much for the movies. Not only did I have to go bowling with him, but I had to teach him how. Please don't let anyone from school be there, I prayed.

Chapter Two

I saw three kids from school as soon as we walked in the door. Or should I say, *I* walked in the door. Frank tripped on his shoelace. He stumbled through the doorway.

Some entrance. I hurried over to the shoe-rental desk. Maybe I'd lose Frank along the way. But when I got to the desk, Frank was right behind me.

Nothing went wrong for at least five minutes. We got our shoes and our lane. I showed Frank how to pick out a ball. I showed him how to score. Then it was time to show him how to bowl.

He dropped the first ball. It bounced and rolled into the channel. The second ball landed on his foot. His face turned green. I helped him sit down.

I knocked over eight pins in my first frame. The woman in the next lane gave me the thumbs-up sign. I grinned. She looked like a pro. She even had her own ball.

Scott waved at me from two lanes down. He's in my class at school. He was with his older twin brothers, Jake and Jeremy, and two other kids from class. Jake bowled a clean strike.

I sighed and turned back to Frank. His face was its normal color again.

"The idea is to swing your arm back," I explained. I showed him.

"Then move it directly down and forward. Then straighten your fingers and let go. The ball will roll along the lane."

"That sounds easy," Frank said.

He stood up and limped over to his ball. He picked it up with the wrong fingers. I held it for him, and he got his fingers into the right holes.

He hobbled to the lane. I sat on the bench. I was ready to do my best coaching.

"Swing your arm back," I said in a half whisper. I hoped Scott and his brothers couldn't hear me.

Frank followed my directions. He swung his arm back. It went up almost straight behind him.

"Now bring it forward and let go," I hissed.

The next few seconds were endless. Some kind of time warp took over. Frank's arm swung slowly down and forward. His arm went out in front of him. It pointed straight at the lane.

Now, I said in my head. Open your fingers and let go.

Frank did. Unfortunately, at that moment his feet turned to the left. So did his arm. The ball sailed sideways.

The woman in the next lane hit the floor. In the lane beside hers, Scott backed up quickly. He had been ready to bowl.

I watched in horror as the ball floated over the two lanes. Then it bounced off the ball return and changed direction. It sailed into Scott's lane and fell on the wooden floor. It rolled down the lane and knocked over all ten pins.

"It's a strike!" Scott shouted. Jake and Jeremy began to cheer.

Even the woman in the next lane clapped from where she lay on the floor. The whole

bowling center was in an uproar. They laughed and cheered. Frank raised his arms over his head. You'd think he'd just won the World Series. I slunk down on the bench. I wished I were somewhere else.

For the next half hour, people kept coming over. They congratulated Frank on his strike. I played out my game. I won't even talk about my score. Frank wisely decided to give up for the day. The center manager said he wished he had a picture of the whole thing. He told Frank to make sure to come back soon.

It won't be with me, I thought. I'm never coming back here. And Mom wanted Frank and me to play in the father-son game? No way.

Chapter Three

As I said before, my mother didn't understand. Neither did Toby.

"What difference does it make?" Mom said. "So he's not the world's best bowler."

"I wonder what the chances are of that happening," Toby said. "I wish I'd been there."

Why couldn't they see that I'd been humiliated? I was one of the top athletes in school, and my stepfather couldn't hold on to a bowling ball. I wished my father were still around. He'd probably scored 300 games every week.

I still hadn't figured out how to avoid the father-son game. I had three weeks left. I was considering getting chicken pox. Or moving to Alaska.

Then things got worse.

"How would you like to take Frank shopping?" Mom asked on Tuesday night.

I'd rather go to the dentist.

"It'll give you and Frank a chance to spend some time together," she said quickly.

I made a face. I'd tried to stop myself, but my face has a mind of its own sometimes.

"You can go to Geisler's afterward," she said.

My mother isn't above bribery. She knows my favorite thing in the world is a hot-fudge sundae with peanut butter and chocolate ice cream, topped with walnuts. And only Geis-ler's makes it.

I nodded reluctantly. Besides, maybe it would take her mind off the father-son game.

"Frank needs some jeans for the father-son game," Mom added. "He doesn't own any."

Somehow that didn't surprise me.

I talked Toby into going. The mall was crowded for a weeknight. Inside Jeans Plus, the racks of clothes went on for miles. Frank looked confused. As usual, the salesclerks were all out to dinner or something.

"What color do you want?" I asked.

Frank hesitated. "Well, jeans color, I guess. You know—blue?"

It was a start.

"What size?" I said.

That, at least, he knew. "Forty-two waist," he said.

I wondered if they made them that big.

"Okay," I said. "Toby, you start with that rack and I'll do this one."

"What about me?" Frank said.

I had visions of him knocking over one of the racks, and us spending the rest of the night picking up large pants.

"We'll only be a minute," I said. "Then you can try them on."

Toby had already disappeared into the racks. His head didn't clear the tops, but soon I heard a muffled voice. "Here's one," the voice said.

The clothes moved, and Toby came out clutching a pair of dark blue jeans.

I hustled Frank off to the dressing room. I even took the jeans off the hanger, so he wouldn't hurt himself on the clips. Then Toby and I hung around outside by the mirrors, trying to see who could make the worst faces.

I had just created a masterpiece when

Frank appeared in the mirror behind me. He was walking stiff-legged. The jeans were bunched up around his feet and ankles.

Maybe now we could get out of here.

"They look great," I said.

Toby gave me a strange look.

"They're a little stiff," Frank said. "I can't bend my knees."

"You need a pair of prewashed," Toby chimed in. "This kind takes forever to soften up."

Toby disappeared into the racks again. He came back with a pair of soft, light blue pants.

"Here," he said breathlessly. "Try these."

"You should get a job here," Frank said to Toby. "You're good at this."

Toby grinned. He likes being helpful.

When Frank came out of the dressing room this time, he walked more normally. For him, that is. His knees could bend, and he looked as if he wouldn't be afraid to sit down. The jeans were still bunched up around his ankles.

"These are great," Frank said. "Real comfortable."

Toby looked at the ankles. "They're a little . . ." He hesitated. Toby was always careful when he talked about other people's height. "They're a little long," Toby finally got out. "Maybe we can find something"—he almost choked on the word—"shorter."

"I'll have them taken up," Frank said. "I wouldn't want to trip on them during the father-son softball game. I've never played in one before. Besides," he added with a laugh, "when you're my height, you get used to having pants taken up."

Toby's jaw dropped. You could tell he was surprised that someone could be so casual about being short. Frank's height didn't seem to bother Frank at all.

DRESSING
ROOMS

LARGE

MEDIUM

SMALL

"They promised me a growth spurt," Frank said.

Toby nodded. He knew what that meant. His father was always telling him he'd grow all at once when he got older.

"The spurt never came," Frank said. "But there are advantages. I'm the last one to get wet in a rainstorm."

He winked at Toby, and Toby burst out laughing.

Frank went back to the dressing room to change, tripping over the pants all the way.

"The only thing good about this day will be Geisler's," I said.

"Frank's all right," Toby said. "He's a good sport."

"He's not *your* stepfather," I said. "Everybody notices when he does stupid things. And says stupid things."

"It doesn't seem to bug anyone but you," Toby said.

Geisler's didn't turn out to be so good, after all. The hot fudge melted the ice cream too fast, and they were out of walnuts. Toby and Frank spent the whole time telling each other corny jokes. I didn't finish the sundae. I just let it melt.

It can't get worse, I thought.

Chapter Four

Juliet was fully trained now. Frank would come into the room. Juliet would go behind the couch. She'd come out when he sat down. Then she wanted her ears rubbed.

Mom wasn't so lucky. Two of her best glasses were gone forever. She was getting good at persuading Frank not to help with the dishes. The little rug from the living room was now in my room. And peeling vegetables had become my permanent job.

But Mom wouldn't give up. She kept pushing Frank and me together.

On Thursday, Toby and I had just come back from playing basketball. We play with Scott and the twins. We use the driveway of the old grocery store on the corner. Years ago, someone had put up a hoop there. The driveway backs onto Mrs. Cramer's house. After a while, she had yelled at us to go home. She always does that.

"You guys playing again tomorrow night?" Mom asked.

I made a sound to cover up a definite answer.

"Why not ask Frank?" she said.

"No!" I exploded. "None of the other kids ask their fathers."

"Just this once," she said. "Just this time. You might even have fun."

Sure, I thought. Frank probably played basketball the way he bowled. We'd all wind up in the hospital.

The guys didn't seem to mind when I dragged Frank along. I think Toby was glad to have someone around who didn't tower over him. And, for a change, Scott wasn't the worst player. I'm sure he liked that.

At least Frank didn't tease Jake and Jeremy. Parents always say they look alike. But after thirty seconds you can see that they don't at all. Frank got their names straight right off. That impressed them.

I explained the rules to Frank. Then I tossed the ball to Toby. Toby tossed it to Scott. Scott threw it to me. I threw it to Frank. Frank, of course, missed it.

The ball bounced out into the street. It took him a few minutes to get it. He had to wait for the traffic.

I didn't throw the ball to Frank again. He

28

was going to make a fool out of me. I didn't want to help him do it.

Then Scott made a fatal play. He threw the ball to Frank. Frank galloped for the basket. Jake charged him. When Jake was almost on him, Frank threw the ball, hard and wild. The ball bounced off the building. It slammed into Mrs. Cramer's kitchen window.

We froze. We had been playing there for years. We had never even hit her house.

She came shrieking to the back door. "I'm calling the police," she yelled. "Delinquents, all of you. No sense of responsibility. I know who you are. You won't get away with this."

She peered into the evening light and spotted Frank.

"Who are you?" she said. "I don't know you."

Frank stepped forward. "I'm Frank Latham," he said. "Matt is my stepson. I broke the window. I'll be glad to pay for it."

Mrs. Cramer hesitated. Then she came out onto the back stoop. "Well, at least some parents know what their children are doing," she said grudgingly. "It's not easy living alone."

"It must be a worry," Frank agreed.

"People always try to take advantage of an old woman," she said.

Frank nodded sympathetically. That started Mrs. Cramer on a bunch of complaints. The rest of us stood and shuffled our feet.

"Have that window fixed and send the bill to me," Frank said finally. "I'll stop by to see how you're doing."

An awful thing happened next. Mrs. Cramer smiled. Her lips cracked open over wide gaping holes between her teeth. The wrinkles around her mouth tripled in number.

"Thank you, Mr. Latham," she said. "You're a true gentleman. And, next time, you and the boys stop in for cookies."

Frank said good night and picked up the ball.

"I don't know how you did it, Frank," Scott said. We rounded the corner of the grocery store. "I thought we were in for it," he added.

"She would've called the police," Jeremy said. "Our father would never have let us out again."

"I'd be grounded for life," Toby agreed. "Want to play again tomorrow night, Frank?"

Frank glanced at me, and I looked away. "I don't think basketball is my game," he said. "But thanks for the offer."

The others went off. Frank and I walked home in silence. My mother's great ideas were making my life miserable.

Chapter Five

"Maybe you and Frank could go to a movie," my mother said on Sunday afternoon.

"That's a great idea!" I said.

She looked at me in surprise.

It was more than great. It was brilliant. Mom was finally catching on that Frank was too klutzy to play sports. But if we went someplace where he only had to sit and watch—what could happen?

I wouldn't have to go to Alaska. My mother would be happy that we were doing something together. And maybe she'd forget the father-son game.

Everything started off okay. I bought a lot of stuff to eat. That way, we didn't have to talk much. And the theater was almost empty. No one from school was around to see us together.

"Hey, Matt."

It was Toby and Scott and the twins. Naturally. And here I was, hanging around with my stepfather on a Sunday afternoon.

"I called to see if you wanted to come with us," Toby said, "but your mother said you had left already."

They filed into the row in front of us, turning around to talk about the movie. No one had seen it yet. It was supposed to be good. It was a comedy about a high-school kid who accidentally winds up on Jupiter. He gets into trouble with the aliens. They want to do experiments on him.

It was my kind of movie. But I picked it because I figured an adult wouldn't like it. And if Frank really hated it, maybe he'd stop going along with Mom's ideas about us doing things together.

Frank had finished the last of the popcorn when it started. The laughing, I mean. I had never heard Frank laugh before. I had seen him smile. And I had heard him chuckle. He did that a lot, especially when he was teasing Mom about something. But laugh? No. I had never heard him laugh.

It turned out that Frank has one of those laughs that you hear sometimes in a movie theater. You always feel sorry for the people who are sitting near the guy.

It started off as an occasional snort. Then it grew into a series of honkings. Between the honkings came gasping, and a kind of hiccup.

At first, I thought he had some popcorn stuck in his throat. Then I looked at him in the light from the screen. I could see tears running down his face.

I have to admit that the movie was funny. And Toby and Scott and the twins were laughing. I was laughing, too. But I certainly wasn't making a spectacle of myself.

Then I noticed something strange. Frank's laugh was contagious. And it wasn't affecting only Toby and Scott and his brothers. Everyone in the theater was laughing.

Frank would start laughing. Then Toby would join in. Scott and the twins would pick it up. Soon the whole theater was in an uproar. The more everyone else laughed, the less I did. I mean, it wasn't that funny. Maybe they were laughing at Frank.

I hunkered down in my seat and thought about Alaska. I couldn't concentrate on the movie at all. I just waited for Frank to laugh, and for the waves of laughter that would follow. At one point, Jeremy actually fell off his

seat and into the aisle. And Scott was holding his stomach as if he was in pain.

It was a long movie. It went on forever. When the lights finally came on, Frank stood up, wiping his eyes.

"Great movie," he said. "Best one I've seen in a long time."

So much for my choice of movies.

"Did you ever see *Vacation on Mars?*" Scott asked him. "You'd love it."

"Yeah," agreed Jake. "We'll have to rent the video some night, Frank. You can come over to our house to see it."

Okay, so they weren't laughing at Frank. But they didn't have to invite him over.

They all walked out ahead of me, talking about the movie. Toby and Scott and Frank took turns acting out some of the funnier parts. Nobody seemed to notice that I wasn't laughing. Nobody seemed to notice me at all.

Chapter Six

"The father-son game is a week from Saturday," Mom announced one evening.

I was peeling carrots. Mom had convinced Frank to watch the news.

"I'm not going," I said.

I thought she'd get mad. All she did was sit down. She stared at some chicken parts she'd placed in a pan.

There was a long silence.

"Okay," she said. "If that's the way you feel."

Suspicious, I glanced at her. "Do you mean it?" I said, not daring to breathe.

"Yes, I mean it," she said. "I've hoped and hoped that you and Frank would become friends. I guess it's impossible. You're too different. I'm not going to force you."

When anger doesn't work, Mom tries guilt. And I did feel guilty. I knew Mom loved Frank, even if I didn't. And our lives *had* been better since they'd met. Mom was happier, that was for sure. The little frown between her eyes had disappeared. And Juliet was happy. She loved all the attention. I was the one who was spoiling everything.

Mom was right, though. Frank and I had nothing in common. We could live together. But no rule said we had to like each other, or do things together.

After dinner, I washed the dishes and left

them to dry. Frank came in and sat at the kitchen table. He began taking apart a pair of binoculars.

"What are you doing?" I asked.

"Cleaning these binoculars," Frank said.

"What do you do with them?" I asked. I put the last pot on the drainboard and leaned against the counter.

"They help me look at birds," Frank said.

I stifled a snort. It seemed like such a stupid thing to do—watch birds. And boring.

"My bird club is doing some banding on Saturday," Frank said. "How about going with me?"

Frantically, I tried to think of an excuse, but my mind went blank. A delaying tactic would have to do. "What's banding?" I asked.

"We catch birds and put numbers on their legs, on small tags," Frank said. "Then we let them go. A lot of information comes in when the birds are spotted again."

Talk about boring. But I still couldn't come up with a good excuse.

Frank looked up at me. "You've been showing me the things you like to do," he said. "Now it's my turn. I'll show you something I like to do."

Frank was right. He had been trailing me around, trying to do things he couldn't do. If nothing else, as Toby said, he was a good sport. I couldn't take a double dose of guilt in one night.

"Okay," I said. "I'll try it."

"We have to get up at six," Frank said. "Birds like the early-morning hours."

I choked back a sound. I'd never been up at six in my life. I regretted this already.

Chapter Seven

The sun was just coming up when we drove to the state park. Frank introduced me to the other people at the nature center. Then we set out across the field.

I was a few steps ahead of Frank when this huge cobwebby thing wrapped itself around my face. My arms flailed out, trying to get it off.

"Stand still," Frank said. "You're caught in the net."

He unwrapped me. Then he showed me the big net that hung across the field. It was made of very fine thread to catch the birds.

I felt like a jerk. But Frank only said, "It's hard to see it."

Frank checked that it was set up okay. Then we headed back to the building. We sat down outside with the others and waited. Nobody said a word. They sure were unfriendly. Frank fell asleep.

I started to dig a hole in the dirt with the toe of my shoe. Maybe I could get to Alaska that way.

After a few minutes, I noticed a couple of people staring at me.

Frank stirred and poked me. "You're whistling," he said.

I shrugged. "So what?"

"You'll scare the birds," Frank said.

My face got hot. Now I really felt like

a jerk. And here I thought the people were unfriendly.

I shut up and tried to make the hole I was digging big enough to crawl into.

After about an hour, we headed for the net. It was a waste of time. I hadn't seen one bird, and I had been watching.

I couldn't believe it! There must have been twenty birds along the net. The first one had its claws twisted in the net, and it hung at an angle. Its wings flapped as it tried to get loose.

While I watched, Frank freed the bird from the net. It seemed easy enough. He put the bird in a paper bag and moved on.

"Think you can handle this one?" he asked. He pointed to a tiny black-and-white bird. "It's a chickadee."

"No problem," I said.

Frank moved down the net.

I grabbed the bird on top of its wings, the

way Frank had shown me. With my left hand, I began to unwind the threads from its claws. The first thread came off easily. But the second looped around both claws. The more I tried to unwind the thread, the more it twisted around the bird's legs.

The bird struggled against my hand. My thumb slipped off its wing. Now its wing was caught on the threads, too. Little pieces of feathers flew into my face.

I started to sweat. What if I couldn't get the bird off the net? Would they have to kill it or something? Where was Frank?

"Frank!" I yelled.

Frank was there in an instant. How he got across that field so fast, I have no idea. He eased his fingers around the bird. I took my hand away and put it in my pocket. I didn't want Frank to see it shaking. "It got more and more tangled," I said.

Frank's fingers moved quickly. First he freed the chickadee's wing. Then he went to work on its claws and legs.

It took only seconds for Frank to unravel the bird. With one finger, he stroked the top of the bird's head.

"It's okay."

He held the bird out to me. I stroked it as I had seen Frank do. It sure was soft.

"Let's go get these banded," Frank said.

Inside the building, Frank clipped a metal tag around the chickadee's leg. The bird didn't seem to mind at all. Frank wrote its number and the word "chickadee" in a log book.

After Frank finished the banding, we took the bags out back and he let the birds go. "You do this one," he said, handing me the chickadee.

I took the chickadee from the bag. I held my arm out and opened my hand. The bird didn't move. "He's hurt or something," I said.

"It's a defense," Frank said. "Turn your hand upside down."

"But he'll fall off," I said.

"As soon as he feels himself falling, he'll start to fly."

I held my breath and turned my hand upside down. Sure enough, the bird flew off to the woods. What I didn't know about birds could fill a book.

Frank and I drove home in our usual silence, but it felt different this time. Frank was a klutz about sports and dishes and Juliet's tail. I was a klutz when it came to birds. We were different, all right. But maybe the father-son softball game wouldn't be so bad, after all.

Chapter Eight

That father-son softball game will go down in the annals of Dent Elementary School. I'll tell you right now that the Red team won—ours. But it wasn't who won that was important. It was the way we won. And it was all because of Frank.

Frank didn't look bad in his red T-shirt and new jeans and red hat. The T-shirt stretched a little too much over his stomach. But the cap covered his bald spot. When he ran, he sort of clumped along. This was the same person who had flown like the wind to rescue a tied-up bird.

Toby and his dad were on the Red team, too. Scott was on the Blue team. The score was even until the last inning. Then the Reds scored a run.

When it was their turn at bat, the Blues went all out to tie the game. Scott himself was on second base. He was ready to run if the batter could connect with the ball. With two outs, he didn't have much of a chance.

I was covering third base for the Reds. The coach knew I could play. He knew I was fast. With the right ball, I could tag Scott out. The game would be over.

The count was three balls and two strikes on the batter. I had seen this kid play before. He was a big guy. He seemed to play best in a pinch. I knew he was going to hit that ball. With any luck, it would come my way.

Luck had nothing to do with what happened next. The kid hit the ball all right. It headed toward left field. I started running back, sure I could make it. It was high. At the last second, I leaped and stretched. The ball sailed over my head. When I came down, one foot got in the way of the other. I sat down hard, facing left field.

I could see Frank standing there. Yes, standing there. He didn't seem to understand what was happening. His right hand was up over his eyes. His cap was set back on his head. It would take him at least an hour to get moving. If he ever decided to.

The ball was coming right at him. He just watched it, as if it weren't the least bit important. The people on the sidelines were shouting. I could swear I heard my mother yelling, "Frank, look out!"

"Get the ball, Frank!" I hollered. I knew he couldn't hear me above the noise.

The ball had almost reached Frank. He was still frozen. Then I realized that the ball was going to go over Frank's head. Thank goodness he was short. At least it wouldn't hit him.

That was when Frank moved. He touched his hand to the brim of his cap. He swept the cap off his head. He stretched his arm up, and plop! the ball landed in Frank's cap as if it had been directed by radar.

The game was over. The Reds cheered and yelled and screamed and gathered around Frank. The Blues yelled and screamed and gathered around the umpire. They insisted that the catch was illegal.

The people in the stands shouted and laughed. A few of them started to chant, "Frank, Frank." My mother ran out onto the field. She was laughing so hard, tears were running down her face.

I did the only thing I could do. I ran out to Frank. I slapped him on the back. And I

cheered and yelled with Toby and the rest of the Reds.

As Toby says, Frank's a good sport. He's willing to try things, and he's good with people. And with birds. So what if he can't play sports? My mother likes him, and so does Juliet, and so do my friends. And so do I. It's really not so bad having a klutz for a stepfather.